# Amelia Chamelia

# Amelia Chamelia
## and the Gelato Surprise

Laura Sieveking

illustrations by

Alyssa Bermudez

PUFFIN BOOKS

PUFFIN BOOKS
UK | USA | Canada | Ireland | Australia
India | New Zealand | South Africa | China

Penguin Books is part of the Penguin Random House group of companies
whose addresses can be found at global.penguinrandomhouse.com.

Penguin
Random House
Australia

First published by Penguin Random House Australia Pty Ltd, 2019

Text copyright © Laura Sieveking 2019
Illustrations copyright © Alyssa Bermudez 2019

The moral right of the author and the illustrator has been asserted.

A catalogue record for this
book is available from the
National Library of Australia

ISBN: 978 0 14379 160 7

Cover and internal illustrations by Alyssa Bermudez
Cover design by Ngaio Parr
Internal design and typesetting by Midland Typesetters, Australia
Printed in Australia by Griffin Press, an accredited ISO AS/NZS 14001:2004
Environmental Management System printer

Penguin Random House Australia uses papers that are natural, renewable
and recyclable products and made from wood grown in sustainable forests.
The logging and manufacturing processes are expected to conform to the
environmental regulations of the country of origin.

penguin.com.au

*For Evie and Arianwen*

*Amelia has a secret power. A power
that nobody else knows about.
When she is furious or frightened,
she can change colour.
She can blend into her surroundings.
And when she changes, she cannot be
seen. She becomes invisible.
She is different.
She is special.
She is Amelia Chamelia.*

# 1

# The New Boy

It was a hectic Monday morning at the Chamelia house. After a long summer, the first day back at school had everyone in a tizz.

'Muuuuuum!' wailed Oliver from the top of the stairs. 'I can't find my school hat.'

'Here it is, silly,' laughed Amelia. She handed her little brother his

brand-new Ferntree Grove Primary
hat. 'You left it in the bathroom.'

'Thanks, Amelia.' He placed the hat
on his head, pulled the drawstring up
around his chin and grinned. 'What do
you think?'

'Very smart,' said Amelia. 'Come on,
let's go downstairs, we don't want to
be late.'

In the kitchen Mum was busy preparing packed lunches while Dad was feeding Clare, the baby of the family, her vegemite soldiers. Percy, Amelia's cheeky puppy, was patiently sitting beneath Clare's highchair hoping a few crumbs might fall in his direction.

'Oh, Oliver, look at you in your uniform. I can't believe it's your first day of Kindergarten!' gasped Mum.

Oliver wrinkled his nose and tried to wriggle free as Mum grabbed him for a hug.

'Don't worry, Mum. I'll take care of him,' said Amelia. 'Now that I'm in Year 3 I'm pretty much a grown-up.'

'You sure are, kiddo,' chuckled Dad.

Just as Mum handed Amelia and Oliver their lunchboxes, the doorbell rang.

'Willow's here,' yelled Amelia. She kissed Dad goodbye and ran down the hallway. Amelia yanked the door open and greeted her friend with a hug. The two girls always made the short walk up the road to school together.

'Hi, Amelia,' giggled Willow. 'Are you ready to go?'

Oliver zoomed towards the front door with his oversized schoolbag on his back, grinning from ear to ear. 'I'm ready!'

'Well, someone's excited for their first day of Kindy,' laughed Willow.

'Morning, Willow,' said Mum. She glanced at her watch. 'Gosh – is that the time. We better get going.'

It wasn't long before they arrived at the school gates. Mum dropped Oliver off at Kindergarten and Amelia and Willow skipped across the playground to find their classmates.

Amelia had been looking forward to getting back to school all summer. The end of last year had been crazy – she finally turned eight AND she discovered she had an amazing superpower. She hadn't dared tell anyone other than Percy about how she could turn invisible. But now they were back at school she was thinking about telling Willow.

The problem was, Amelia had no idea how to control her power. She hadn't changed colour since her birthday party before the holidays, despite trying every day to make it happen.

'Amelia! Willow! Over here!' shouted an excited voice from across the playground. It was their best friend, Helen. She was sitting on the grass with their other friends Matthew and Arlo. 'Have you heard?'

'Heard what?' asked Willow.

'Apparently, we've got a new kid joining our class,' said Arlo.

'It's true, I overheard Mrs Hopper telling my mum when we dropped my little sister off at Kindy,' said Helen. 'Sophie was nervous about her first day so Mum wanted to wait in reception until she settled in.'

'A new kid? This is so exciting,' said Amelia. 'And don't worry about Sophie, she'll be fine. Oliver's in her class so at least she has a friend with her.'

Amelia and Willow sat down and all the friends chatted about their summer holidays until the bell rang for the first lesson of the day.

Mrs Ward was standing at the front of the classroom with a big smile on her face as the children filed in from the playground and took their seats. Amelia and Willow loved Mrs Ward and they were so pleased to have her as their class teacher.

'Good morning, 3W,' said Mrs Ward.

'Good morning, Mrs Ward,' chorused the children.

'Welcome back, everyone. I hope you all had a wonderful summer break and you're ready for the new term. Now, before we start, I have some exciting news.' Mrs Ward waved her hand at the door. A small boy with jet black hair shuffled inside.

Curious whispers filled the room.

'We have a new student who will be joining our class,' continued Mrs Ward. 'Everyone, this is Harry Truffle. He has moved here all the way from England. Harry, can you tell us something about your hometown?'

There was an awkward pause. Harry looked around the room and his

cheeks went pink.
He stared down
at his feet and
plunged his hands
deep into his pockets.

'Um. No, not really,'
mumbled Harry.

Mrs Ward frowned
and then quickly
smiled. 'That's okay.
How about you find a
seat. There's a spare spot over there
next to Matthew. Everybody, let's give
Harry a warm Ferntree Grove Primary
welcome!'

The whole class clapped and Harry
made his way to the back of the room
to take his seat. Amelia could tell he
was nervous. She smiled at him as he

walked past, but he didn't take his eyes off the floor.

Throughout the rest of the lesson Amelia peered over at Harry, but his expression never changed, his face was fixed in an angry scowl. As soon as the bell rang for morning break he rushed out of the room without saying a word.

*There's something very curious about this new boy, Harry Truffle,* thought Amelia.

# 2

# Mrs Templeton's Shop

The sun was still blazing down when
the bell rang for the end of the school
day. Amelia and her friends rushed
across the playground to the gates
where Amelia's mum was waiting with
Oliver and Helen's little sister, Sophie.
Amelia's mum always picked them
all up from school and walked them
home. Ferntree Grove was a small

town and Amelia loved that she lived so close to her friends.

'Hey, kids. I was thinking, before I drop each of you home, would you like an ice-cream from Templeton's?' asked Mum.

Amelia, Willow and Helen all gave an excited cheer and Matthew and Arlo high-fived.

Templeton's was one of Amelia's favourite places in town. It was owned by the much-loved Mrs Templeton and the store had been in her family for generations. Everyone in town shopped there – it had everything from party decorations and stationery to flowers and, best of all, ICE-CREAMS!

'I'll take that as a yes then,' chuckled Mum. 'Oliver? Sophie?

Shall we get some ice-cream to celebrate your first day of Kindergarten?'

Oliver beamed and nodded frantically, but Sophie just shrugged and sighed.

'What's up, Sophie?' asked Helen. 'How was your first day?' She held her little sister's hand as they walked along the footpath.

Sophie shrugged again and stared down at the ground.

'Well, you'll feel better after some ice-cream and you can tell us all about Kindy,' said Helen.

As they made their way to Templeton's, the hum of the summer bees filled the air. Amelia was so happy to be back at school with her friends and now she couldn't wait to pick out her favourite rainbow flavour ice-cream.

*TING-A-LING.*

The children ploughed through the door. After the short walk they were relieved to be in the cool shop. Oliver ran straight to the ice-cream counter, balancing on his tiptoes to examine the delicious flavours.

'Afternoon – how are we all today?' asked Mrs Templeton.

'I've just done my first day of
big school and now we're going to
have ice-cream!' exclaimed Oliver.

'Well that sounds like the perfect
way to celebrate.' Mrs Templeton
was an older lady with white curls
and a round, smiling face. Her glasses
perched on the end of her little nose
and her dark grey eyes sparkled.
'What about you, Sophie? Are you
happy to finally be at school with
your sister?'

'No,' said Sophie, flatly.

Helen nudged her little sister.
'Sophie – don't be rude!'

'No, thank you,' corrected Sophie.

Mrs Templeton laughed such a
jolly laugh that her whole body
shook as she chuckled. 'Now, go

and choose your ice-creams and take
a seat.'

Amelia's mum paid at the counter
and they went to sit at the table in the
window.

'Sophie, why don't you like school?'
asked Willow.

'I just don't like it. I want to go back
to my preschool.'

'But school is so fun,' said Amelia.
'Most of your friends are at Ferntree
Grove Primary with you, and Oliver is
in your class.'

Sophie shuffled uncomfortably
in her seat. 'Oliver loves Kindy.
But I just want to go back to Miss
Little. I want to play in my preschool
playground and have nap time in the
afternoon.'

'I agree,' said Arlo in between licks. 'Preschool is awesome. You don't even do any work. You just run around and play all day.'

Everyone around the table burst out laughing and then . . .

*TING-A-LING*.

Someone walked through the door. Amelia looked up and saw Harry Truffle stroll into the shop with his dad. Amelia waved at Harry, but he turned away and hid his face behind the comic book he was reading.

'Good afternoon,' said Harry's dad in a cheery English accent.

'Mr Truffle, lovely to see you again. Are you settling in okay?' asked Mrs Templeton.

'Yes, thanks. We're still getting used to this summer heat though. When we left England it was snowing! I think we need an ice-cream to cool us down, don't we, Harry? Which flavour would you like, son?'

Harry closed his comic book and peered over the counter at the selection.

'Do you have butterscotch?' mumbled Harry.

'Afraid not, but we do have caramel, which is quite similar,' said Mrs Templeton.

Harry frowned. 'No, that's okay. I don't want anything.'

Harry buried his nose back in his comic and plodded towards the shop door. Amelia tried to smile at him again, but Harry's face remained as cold as her ice-cream.

After dinner that evening Amelia cuddled up to Percy on the beanbag in her room and jotted down the day's events in her special diary. Willow had given it to her for her eighth birthday and Amelia made sure she wrote in it every day.

Amelia flicked back to the first entry about her birthday party and her secret power. She sighed and closed the book. 'Oh, P. I wish I knew how to control my power. I need it to happen again so I can understand what's going on. Maybe then I could tell Willow.'

Percy grumbled and nudged her hand.

'You're right, P. I should concentrate on writing about my first day back at school.' Amelia tickled Percy's tummy and opened her diary again.

'Oh! I forgot to tell you. A new boy started today, his name's Harry Truffle. He's not friendly at all though. In fact, I think he's pretty rude and mean. There's something fishy about him.'

Amelia's puppy began to snore as he drifted off to sleep.

'I think I'd better keep a close eye on this Truffle kid,' said Amelia as she yawned. She was exhausted after her first day back at school, so Amelia locked her diary, hid the key in her music box and hopped into bed.

As soon as Amelia's head hit the pillow she was fast asleep, dreaming about her power and camouflaging into the colours of her favourite rainbow ice-cream.

# 3

# An Exciting
# Announcement

'Again! *Uno, due, tre.*'

'*Uno, due, tre,*' recited the
children.

One of the reasons Amelia had been
so excited to go back to school was
because at Ferntree Grove Primary,
when you reached Year 3, you started
language lessons. Today was their first
ever Italian lesson and Amelia's class

were learning how to count with
Mr Russo.

'*Molto bene*! Very good, everyone,'
said Mr Russo. 'You can now count to
three in Italian.'

'I think Italian is my new favourite
lesson,' whispered Amelia to
Willow.

'The thing I love most about Italy
is the food,' continued Mr Russo.
'Can anyone think of some famous
Italian foods?' He laughed as hands
shot up all around the classroom.

'Pasta!' called out Matthew.

'Pizza!' exclaimed Willow. 'It's my
favourite.'

'You and me both, Willow,' agreed
Mr Russo. 'Can anyone think of
others?'

'What about coffee? My mum *always* has a cappuccino in the morning,' said Helen.

'Yes, Helen. Italy is known for its fabulous coffee. But there is one popular Italian food none of you have mentioned yet.' Mr Russo grinned. 'I'll give you a clue: it's very cold and excellent to have on a hot day.'

Amelia knew immediately and waved her hand in the air. 'Ice-cream, ice-cream!'

'Well done, Amelia,' said Mr Russo. 'However, in Italy it's a special type of ice-cream with a special name. It starts with a G.'

'Ooh, ooh, I know,' said Helen. 'Is it gelato?'

'*Brava*, Helen. Gelato is Italian ice-cream. Next week we are going to learn the Italian names for some delicious flavours and how to order them in Italian.'

'I wish we could eat gelato instead of just talk about it,' moaned Arlo.

'Well, Arlo, you're in luck. I have been planning a very special event with Principal Howe.' Mr Russo pulled out a rolled up poster from his desk drawer. 'Next Friday, Ferntree Grove Primary will be celebrating all things Italian with Gelato Day!'

He pulled open the poster to reveal a picture of a giant ice-cream with the words GELATO DAY, printed across the top.

The class began to chatter loudly.

'The whole school will be taking part in this event so you'll be seeing a few of these fabulous posters

dotted around the playground and noticeboards.'

The room was abuzz with excitement, and then the bell for lunchbreak cut through the noise.

'Before you rush off I have one more announcement. For this special day to go ahead the whole school must be on their best behaviour over the next week. That means each and every one of you – including me!' chuckled Mr Russo. 'But in all seriousness, Principal Howe has made it very clear, if anyone gets up to any mischief or she gets even a whiff of naughtiness, Gelato Day will be called off.'

'Oh, we'll behave,' assured Amelia. 'We all LOVE gelato. We wouldn't dare to be naughty!'

The entire class bundled out of the classroom, yapping about their favourite gelato flavours.

'I can't wait for Gelato Day!' squealed Willow.

Amelia noticed Harry Truffle hovering by the doorway. 'What about you, Harry? What gelato flavour are you going to pick?'

Harry scowled. 'Gelato Day sounds silly. I don't get why everyone is so excited.' He slung his schoolbag over his shoulder and stomped off across the playground.

'What's up with that new kid?' asked Arlo.

'I don't know,' said Amelia. 'But something seems to have upset him.'

# 4

# The Shocking Thing

It was a drizzly Friday morning in Ferntree Grove. Amelia and Willow linked arms and huddled under Amelia's favourite rainbow umbrella as they walked to school.

'Hey!' called Helen. She stood waiting for them in the playground and was wearing her polka dot gumboots and matching raincoat, protecting her from the summer downpour.

'Hi, Helen. I wish I had some gumboots right now,' whinged Willow. 'I hope it doesn't rain on Gelato Day.'

'Me too,' moaned Amelia. She could feel her soggy socks squelching in her school shoes.

'Even if it does, we'll still be eating yummy gelato,' said Helen. She always managed to be cheerful and positive. Amelia loved that about her.

There was only one week to go until Gelato Day and it was all anyone could talk about.

The girls headed off across the playground to find Arlo and Matthew when they bumped into the school caretaker, Mr Tait. He was struggling

to carry a big bucket filled to the brim
with soapy water. Suds and bubbles
sloshed over the top with every step
he took.

'Good morning, Mr Tait,' chorused
the girls.

'Not such a good morning, I'm
afraid,' grumbled Mr Tait.

'What's the matter?' asked Amelia.
They skipped to keep up with him
as he marched towards the
classrooms.

Mr Tait harrumphed, 'You'll see.'

The girls frowned at each
other, puzzled, as they reached the
Kindergarten classrooms.

Mr Tait put his bucket down and
pointed to the sign in front of them.
'THIS is the problem!'

The girls gasped in shock. The Kindergarten sign had been scribbled on in black marker.

'Who did that?' asked Willow.

Mr Tait pulled a sponge out of the bucket and began to scrub away at the scribbles. 'Beats me. It wasn't here when I opened the gates this morning, and now it is.'

*Who would do such a thing?* thought Amelia.

The girls took a closer look. The person who had done it hadn't written any words – they had just scrawled all over the sign and drawn a frowny face.

'All I know is someone's up to mischief and I don't have time to be cleaning up after GRAFFITI BANDITS,' huffed Mr Tait.

'What's *graffiti*?' asked Helen.

'It's when someone draws all over public property, like this. And it's against the law. I hope our little "artist" here quits now, or they will be in a heap of trouble.'

The sound of the bell pierced the air and the playground became a bustle of children making their way to morning assembly. Willow and Helen set off to join their classmates.

'You coming, Amelia?' they yelled.

'Yeah, be there in a second.' Amelia stared at the scribble. The jagged lines moved angrily all over the sign. Whoever had done this was very cross.

'But who could it be?' whispered Amelia.

By lunchtime the rain had stopped and the sun was shining. Amelia strolled over to the picnic benches where her friends were tucking into their food.

'Amelia, come sit down,' called Willow. 'Helen and I were just telling Matthew and Arlo about the graffiti.'

Amelia perched on the bench and took out her lunchbox. 'I still can't believe that someone from Ferntree Grove Primary could do such a thing. Nothing like this has ever happened before.'

'I know,' agreed Helen. 'Mr Tait was furious.'

'Do you think he'll tell Principal Howe?' asked Willow.

Amelia shrugged. 'He said graffiti was against the law so –'

'Uh-oh,' interrupted Matthew.

'What's the matter, Matthew?' asked Amelia.

'Well, if Principal Howe finds out about the graffiti and that someone at school has not been on their "best behaviour", what do you think she'll do about Gelato Day?'

'Oh dear,' groaned Willow. 'Mr Russo did warn us. He said if Principal Howe gets even a whiff of naughtiness . . .'

'. . . Gelato Day would be called off!' continued Amelia.

'We shouldn't jump to conclusions,' said Helen. 'This graffiti nonsense might be a one off.'

'You're right, Helen,' agreed Arlo. 'Mr Russo wouldn't let Gelato Day get cancelled over one silly scribble.'

Amelia wasn't so sure, but before she could give it more thought, something across the oval distracted her – it was Harry Truffle. He was eating his lunch by himself. Amelia suddenly felt very sad for Harry.

'What are you staring at?' asked Willow.

'It's Harry. He's all alone. I think we should go and eat lunch with him.'

The others didn't seem sure. Since the first day of school, every time they had tried to speak to Harry, or asked him if he wanted to play with them, he had always said no.

'Harry!' yelled Amelia. Her friends looked at her with surprise. 'What? He might say yes this time.'

Willow grinned. 'Come on, let's go ask him.'

Amelia and Willow trotted over to Harry and sat down next to him.

'Hi, Harry. We were wondering if we could eat lunch with you today?' asked Willow. She flashed him her best smile and before he could answer she beckoned the others to come over.

'I-I'm not sure –' began Harry.

'Come on, Harry, we're all here now,' interrupted Willow. 'And my mum packed some lollies for me to share with everyone.' She pulled out a packet of sweeties from her lunchbox.

Harry smiled nervously and then nodded.

'Yay, Harry,' cheered Arlo as he grabbed a bright green chewy snake.

'So, Harry, how do you like Australia?' asked Amelia.

'Erm, yeah – it's okay.' Harry's cheeks turned pink and then he quickly stood up. 'Listen, thanks for coming to sit with me, but I've got to go.'

'Stay a bit, Harry,' said Amelia. 'We were going to play bullrush and thought you'd want to join in?'

'Erm, no, it's okay. I need to go.' He gathered up his lunchbox and comic books and hurried back to the classrooms.

Helen frowned. 'He doesn't like to hang around, does he?'

Amelia glanced at the spot where Harry had been sitting. The sun was reflecting off something shiny.

She leaned over to pick up the object nestled in the grass.

'Is that . . .' began Willow, but she didn't finish her sentence.

Amelia was holding a black marker pen in her hands. Nobody said anything, but they were all thinking the same thing . . .

*Was Harry Truffle the graffiti bandit?*

# 5

# Final Warning

It was Monday morning assembly
and every single student was sitting
cross-legged on the floor in the big
hall. Amelia loved morning assembly
because it was the one time of
day when the whole school, from
Kindergarten to Year 6, was together.
And the best part, they got to sing the
school song!

'Good morning, everyone,' said Principal Howe.

'Good morning, Principal Howe,' chanted the children.

Amelia looked around the hall – she noticed something was different about this morning's assembly. Usually all the teachers would be sitting at the back of the hall, but today they were standing silent and stony-faced on stage behind Principal Howe.

For as long as Amelia had been at Ferntree Grove Primary she had never seen Principal Howe without a smile on her face, but this morning her lips were pursed shut.

Amelia gulped.

Principal Howe straightened her glasses and peered down at the rows of children staring up at her. 'In all my years as principal, I don't think I've ever been more disappointed.'

The hall was so quiet you could have heard a bubble burst.

Principal Howe used a little remote to light up the screen behind her. A photo appeared of the graffiti.

Amelia and Willow exchanged worried glances.

'On Friday morning, Mr Tait came to me with a rather shocking discovery. First, we saw that someone had done this to our Kindergarten sign.' Principal Howe shook her head and clicked the remote once more, changing the photo. 'And then, on Friday afternoon, two more incidents of graffiti were discovered on school property.'

Amelia held her hand to her mouth as she stared at the next photo on the big screen. It was of the brand-new adventure equipment in the playground. There were dark, scribbly lines all the way down the slide. Amelia's mind flashed back to the marker pen Harry had left behind on the school oval the other day.

Principal Howe sighed and pressed the button again. Another image flashed up. It was a door in the girls' toilets with another scribble and frowny face. Everyone in the hall gasped. This was serious.

'Now, we don't know who the culprit is, but we will find out. And in the meantime, if we see ONE more piece of graffiti, Gelato Day will be CANCELLED.'

The hall erupted into worried chatter.

Amelia felt a flash of anger – someone was trying to ruin Gelato Day! All of a sudden, she felt extremely peculiar. And then . . . a chill pulsed through her body – she was freezing.

*Oh no! Not now!*

Amelia remembered this feeling. She was changing!

*I can't change now! Not in front of the entire school!*

She squeezed her eyes shut, hoping she could control her power, but it was no good . . . Her toes *tingled* and her knees *trembled*, then her skin began to *prickle* and her nose started to *tickle*. Her breathing became quicker, and then . . .

'SILENCE!' roared Principal Howe.

Amelia's eyes sprung open in surprise. As everyone went quiet her skin started to warm up. She had been expecting to hiccup and then turn invisible like every other time. But somehow she had managed to stop herself from changing. Relief flooded over Amelia as she looked down at her pink hands and blue school uniform.

'This is your final warning,' continued Principal Howe. 'I'm assuming the graffiti bandit doesn't want to spoil Gelato Day for the whole school. Now, go to class. One more slip-up, and Gelato Day is OFF.'

As the students filed out of the assembly hall, the mood was very heavy. Everybody was worried about Gelato Day being cancelled. Amelia trailed behind her friends as they discussed the graffiti bandit, but all she could think about was how she had managed to control her power.

'Of course,' gasped Amelia. 'Principal Howe made me jump. She made me jump which stopped me hiccupping. Perhaps I didn't turn invisible because I didn't hiccup!'

'What are you mumbling about, Amelia?' asked Willow.

Amelia ran to catch up. 'Oh, nothing – just thinking about who the graffiti bandit could be.'

'We've got to do something to save Gelato Day,' declared Arlo.

Amelia thought for a second – she was determined to work out how to control her power, but first, the graffiti bandit had to be stopped. 'You're right, Arlo. We need an emergency meeting to find out who this troublemaker is.'

'Let's meet at the tennis courts at lunchtime,' said Matthew. 'We can put together a list of suspects – just like real detectives.'

'Good plan,' said Amelia. 'If we figure out who the graffiti bandit is before they strike again, we might be able to save Gelato Day.'

*And after that, I can focus on my superpower*, thought Amelia excitedly.

# 6

# Suspects

As soon as the bell rang for lunchbreak, Amelia and her friends ran to a quiet corner on the tennis courts to discuss the graffiti bandit.

'Thank you for coming to this important emergency meeting,' said Amelia.

'I'll take notes,' chirped Willow. She flipped open her fluffy notebook

and held her pen above the page, ready
to write.

'So, what do we know about the
crime?' asked Helen.

'Mr Tait said he discovered the
first graffiti on the Kindergarten sign
before assembly on Friday, but it
hadn't been there when he opened
the gates that same morning.' Amelia
scratched her chin, something didn't
make sense. 'But only Kindy to
Year 3 are allowed in that part of the
playground in the morning – someone
would have noticed if there was an
older kid hanging around.'

'Good thinking, Amelia. That
narrows it down a little bit,' said Helen.
'So whoever did this is probably in
Kindy to Year 3.'

'What about suspects?' asked Arlo. 'Has anyone seen anybody acting suspiciously?'

Willow turned to a fresh page in her notebook and wrote 'SUSPECTS' in big letters. She glanced up at her friends, ready to jot down the first name.

'What about Harry Truffle?' suggested Helen. 'He's always so cross.'

Matthew nodded in agreement. 'And I don't think he wants to be here one little bit.'

'Also, remember that black marker pen he left on the oval? He totally could have used it for the graffiti,' added Arlo.

'I'm not sure,' said Amelia. 'It must be scary being the new kid. I don't think it's fair to blame Harry just because he had a black marker pen.'

'Well, do we have any other suspects?' huffed Willow.

Everyone looked at each other with blank faces.

'If we want to get to the bottom of this, we're going to need more evidence,' declared Amelia.

'Exactly!' exclaimed Willow. 'Real detectives search out their suspects. We need to examine the whole school and see if the graffiti bandit has left behind any clues.'

They spread out around the playground on the hunt for evidence. Helen rushed to the water fountains.

Nothing. Arlo and Matthew went to
check the cricket nets. Still nothing.
Amelia rifled in the lost property
bin. Again, there was nothing to find.
But it didn't take long before . . .

'Hey, come here,' yelled Willow.

Willow had stopped in front of the
school noticeboard. On the board
were pieces of paper with all kinds
of announcements written on them,
and right in the middle was the big
poster for Gelato Day. She pointed
to the top corner of the poster. Just
above the word 'Gelato' was a black
inky mark.

Amelia gasped. 'Is that what I think
it is?'

'It looks like the beginning of a
scribble,' said Helen.

'Do you think the graffiti bandit was about to draw all over the poster?' asked Matthew.

'Maybe they started but had to stop because a teacher was walking past,' said Arlo.

'It makes sense,' said Willow. 'If the graffiti bandit wants Gelato Day cancelled, what's the one thing they can graffiti that will get instant attention? And the one thing that will remind Principal Howe of her punishment? The poster.'

'So what do we do now?' asked Helen.

'We keep an eye on this poster. If the bandit tried once, they'll try again,' said Amelia. 'And when they do, we'll be ready.'

# 7

# A Pinky Problem

It had been an eventful day, and after the emergency lunchtime meeting Amelia was exhausted and desperate to get home.

'Oh, P. Boy oh boy, do I need to talk to you,' said Amelia. She flopped down on her beanbag and kicked off her school shoes. 'You won't believe what happened today.'

Percy trotted over to Amelia and dropped his chew toy in her lap. He panted and skipped around in circles, hoping for a game of fetch.

Amelia sighed. 'Sorry, P. We can play later. First, I need to tell you about this crazy day.' She shuffled to the side, making room for Percy on the beanbag next to her.

As Amelia told him about the graffiti bandit, how Gelato Day was in danger of being cancelled AND how she almost turned invisible during morning assembly in front of the entire school – faithful Percy sat there, wide-eyed, listening to her every word.

'I don't know what I'd do without you, P.' She tickled his velvet ears and smiled. 'I've been so busy trying to

figure out who the graffiti bandit is,
I haven't had a chance to think about
my powers.'

Percy gave her hand a reassuring lick.

'If I can stop myself turning
invisible, then I must be able to make
myself change as well. But my powers
only work when I'm frightened or
angry,' moaned Amelia.

With a little yip, Percy jumped off the
beanbag. He grabbed her school shoe in
his mouth, growled and shook it as if it
was one of his chew toys.

'Percy!' cried Amelia. 'You naughty
boy. Drop it!'

Percy wagged his tail and danced
around the room, barking and
chucking the shoe up in the air as
Amelia chased him.

*What's the matter with him,* thought Amelia. *Percy knows not to chew shoes.*

As Percy leaped all over the bedroom, Amelia became more and more annoyed.

'I'm not playing, P. You're being a bad dog.'

Percy barked again and jumped up on her neatly made bed, knocking the pillows on the floor.

'Percy! Are you trying to get me in trouble?' shouted Amelia. She dived onto the bed, hoping to catch the cheeky puppy, but he sprung over to the beanbag. Amelia could feel the frustration rising up inside her.

And then it happened. A chill pulsed through her body – she was freezing!

Her toes *tingled* and her knees *trembled*, then her skin began to *prickle* and her nose started to *tickle*.

'P – it's happening!' gasped Amelia.

She squeezed her eyes shut. Her breathing became quicker, and then . . .

HIC –

She hiccupped. It was only a teeny, tiny hiccup, but she knew her power was working.

Percy dropped the shoe and jumped back onto the bed next to Amelia. He nudged her hand and whimpered.

Amelia opened her eyes and stared at her hands, which were resting on her purple bedspread. The fingernail

on her pinky finger was turning a shade of purple.

'Amelia?'

The door opened with a thump, startling Amelia and Percy. She hid her hand under the bedspread as she saw Dad in the doorway.

'What's all the noise about up here?' asked Dad. 'Sounds like a herd of elephants are having a birthday party.'

As Amelia giggled nervously, she could feel her skin warming up. 'Nope, just playing fetch with Percy.'

'Erm, righto, you know how Mum feels about games inside,' warned Dad. 'Running around is for outside.'

Amelia and Percy both nodded.

'Hmmm, I have a niggling feeling you two are up to something. I don't know,' chuckled Dad, 'to be eight again, hey. Well, whatever magic and games you're up to, just keep it down. Okay, kiddo?' He winked and turned to walk out the door.

'Did he just say *magic*?' muttered Amelia. She shook her head, confused, and looked down at her hands as her finger returned to its normal colour.

Percy picked up her school shoe again and wagged his tail.

'Not again, Per –' Amelia paused as she stared at her naughty dog. 'Wait a second. You made me angry on purpose didn't you, Percy?'

He dropped her shoe and gave an excited woof.

Amelia laughed and patted his head. 'That's it! If I want to control

my power I've just got to concentrate
and think of something that makes
me cross.'

Percy playfully danced around
her feet.

'You're a doggy genius!' giggled
Amelia. 'But I don't know how we're
going to explain all the bite marks on
my school shoes to Mum.'

# 8

# Caught in the Act

'Good morning, 3W,' said Mr Russo.
'I know this silly business with the
graffiti bandit has cast a bit of a cloud
over Gelato Day. But after Principal
Howe's final warning can I trust you all
to be on your best behaviour?'

Amelia glanced around as a sea of
heads nodded eagerly. But from the
corner of her eye, right at the back of

the classroom, she noticed one person who wasn't nodding like everyone else – Harry Truffle. He had his head slumped in his hands and was staring outside at the rain.

*What's up with Harry Truffle? He's always so unhappy* . . . thought Amelia as she turned back to the front of the class.

There was one day to go until Gelato Day, and so far, there hadn't been any more graffiti. But that didn't stop Amelia and her friends from keeping an eye out for anyone acting suspiciously.

'Good,' continued Mr Russo. 'Now, as promised I am going to teach you how to order your favourite gelato flavour in Italian.'

Excited chatter filled the room.

'There's *fragola*, which is strawberry. Then there's *cioccolato*, which is . . . can anyone guess?'

'Chocolate!' yelled everyone at once.

'That's right. And then the third flavour is *caramello*, which is caramel. Each of you will be able to go to the gelato stall tomorrow and order one flavour. But remember, you have to order it in Italian.'

'Erm, M-Mr Russo, can I go to the bathroom?' said a quiet voice.

Amelia turned to see Harry with his hand up.

'Yes, Harry, but take a raincoat so you don't get wet when you cross the playground,' replied Mr Russo.

The class continued to recite the Italian words for strawberry, chocolate and caramel as Harry put on his raincoat, pulled the hood over his head and left the room.

Amelia gazed out the window at the dark angry clouds as Mr Russo went around the class asking what flavour was their favourite. Then she frowned. There was a figure outside in the courtyard in a navy raincoat, running across the concrete.

*Is that Harry? Where is he going?* wondered Amelia.

If this was indeed Harry, he was heading in the opposite direction to the toilets.

*I think Harry is up to something. Could he be the graffiti bandit?* thought Amelia. *There's only one way to find out.*

Thinking fast, Amelia waved her hand in the air to get Mr Russo's attention. 'Mr Russo, can I go to the bathroom?'

'Another one? All right, but come back quickly,' tutted Mr Russo.

Amelia grabbed her coat and jogged out of the classroom and into the courtyard. Through the rain she could just about make out the mystery student walking towards the noticeboard that held the Gelato Day poster.

*Is he going to finish the angry
scribble he started?*

Amelia was now convinced she was
hot on the trail of the graffiti bandit.
She was too far away to see what they
were up to, so she crept a little closer.

Hiding herself from view, Amelia
tucked herself around the corner
and leaned up against the courtyard
wall that was painted with the school
mural. It was a bright display of
colours, showing all different types of
Australian wildlife. It had cockatoos
in gumtrees, kangaroos in an orange
desert and colourful fish in the Great
Barrier Reef.

She was still too far away. Amelia
edged along the wall, tiptoeing through
the puddles.

*I can't believe Harry is going to spoil Gelato Day for the whole school.*

Now Amelia was cross. In fact, she wasn't just cross she was FURIOUS! She CLENCHED her fists and STAMPED her foot. As her foot hit the ground she began to feel very peculiar.

Amelia knew exactly what was going to happen next – finally her power was working when she needed it the most!

A chill pulsed through her body – she was freezing! Her toes *tingled* and her knees *trembled*, then her skin began to *prickle* and her nose started to *tickle*. Amelia's breathing became quicker, and then . . .

HICCUP!

She hiccupped. Amelia stared down at her body in amazement as she began to change. Her arms turned a dusty orange, like the sand in the desert on the mural, while her clothes were brown, like the bounding kangaroos behind her. Amelia crept along the wall. To her surprise, her body changed colour with each step she took. As she moved across the bush scene, she camouflaged to match the green gum leaves and the grey koalas.

She moved silently along the wall until she was only a few metres away from the noticeboard. Her skin was now awash with brilliant blues as she leaned against the underwater scene on the wall.

Amelia still couldn't see the face of the culprit, but she was close enough to see them pull a black marker pen from their pocket.

*Hang on a second*, thought Amelia. *That person is far too small to be Harry.*

The graffiti bandit turned again and this time Amelia was close enough to see their face.

Amelia gasped in shock . . .

# 9

# Revealed!

Amelia couldn't believe what she was seeing. She had been expecting it to be the new boy with the jet black hair. But instead she was looking at the blonde curls, big brown eyes and round chubby cheeks of a little girl she'd known for years.

*SOPHIE!*

The graffiti bandit had been Helen's

little sister all along. Amelia was stunned.

Sophie pulled the lid off the marker and lifted it towards the sign.

Suddenly, Amelia felt the anger rush out of her and her skin began to warm up. Her toes *tingled* and her knees *trembled*, then her skin began to *prickle* and her nose started to *tickle*. She saw the pink hues of her skin returning as her breathing became quicker, and then . . .

HICCUP!

She hiccupped.

The sudden noise made Sophie jump with fright.

'Sophie, stop!'

'Amelia! Where did you come from?' exclaimed Sophie.

'It doesn't matter. Are YOU the graffiti bandit?'

The rain came down harder, thumping the concrete below. Sophie's eyes filled with tears. She dropped the marker to the floor.

'Why would you do this?' whispered Amelia.

'Because I hate school,' wailed Sophie. 'I thought if I ruined Gelato Day the teachers would think I was naughty and send me back to preschool.'

Amelia hugged her as she began to cry.

'Am I going to jail?' sobbed Sophie.

'Of course not, silly. But we do need to explain everything to Principal Howe.'

Sophie nodded as Amelia took her by the hand and led her up to Principal Howe's office.

# 10

# Gelato Day

'This is delicious!' said Willow, licking the chocolate gelato off her lips.

The sun was shining and the whole school were sitting on the oval with their gelato.

'Thanks for being so kind to Sophie,' said Helen. 'And for not telling everyone she was the graffiti bandit.'

'That's okay,' replied Amelia. 'I hope she didn't get in trouble?'

'I think Principal Howe was worried instead of angry. She called my parents in and they talked about how much Sophie was missing preschool,' said Helen. 'Mum and Dad had no idea how sad she was, so I think it was good this all happened.'

'Is she okay now?' asked Willow.

'Mum took her back to preschool for a visit. She got to show her old teachers her uniform and they said how proud they were of her for going to big school. She was much happier about everything after that.'

'That's good to hear,' said Willow.

'So, how did you catch her in the act, Amelia?' asked Helen. 'Sophie said

one minute she was alone and then
all of a sudden, you were right next
to her.'

Willow tilted her head to the side
and narrowed her eyes. 'Yeah, how'd
you do that, Amelia?'

'Erm . . . the rain was so loud,
I don't think Sophie heard me,'
said Amelia. Now wasn't the time to let
her secret slip. She could tell Willow
wasn't convinced. Amelia looked
around, keen to change the subject
before Willow asked another question.
'Speaking of cheeky Kindy kids . . .'

Sophie and Oliver skipped over to
Amelia, Helen and Willow.

'Are you having fun today?' asked
Helen.

'Yes!' yelled Oliver and Sophie.

'And guess what?' Sophie beamed.
'My teacher said I was allowed to choose
a special friend to sit with in class to help
me settle in. And I chose Oliver.'

'It's good to have a special friend,
isn't it?' said Willow.

Oliver smiled shyly as Sophie
grabbed his hand. They both ran across
the oval to join their Kindy friends.

'I think everyone deserves a friend,'
said Amelia. She pointed across the
playground to where Harry Truffle was

sitting by himself on a bench with his head in a comic.

Amelia started to walk over to him and Willow and Helen followed.

'Hey, Harry,' said Amelia.

Harry put down his comic book and smiled nervously at the girls. It was then that Amelia noticed Harry wasn't reading, he was in fact *drawing* his own comics.

*Of course, that's why he had a black marker pen – he loves drawing comic books!*

She felt silly for suspecting him of being the graffiti bandit. But that was all in the past now. It was time to make friends with Harry Truffle.

'Wow – I love your drawings,' said Amelia.

Harry's cheeks turned a little pink. 'Thanks.'

'We are going to go find Arlo and Matthew and start a soccer game. Want to come?' asked Amelia.

Harry seemed unsure.

'Is everything okay, Harry? We want to be friends, but we feel like you don't want to hang out with us at all,' said Willow.

'It's not that,' sighed Harry. 'It's just . . . I miss England. My grandparents are still there and I used to see them all the time. They would take me out for butterscotch ice-cream every weekend. And I miss my friends who I've known since Kindergarten. You all seem like such good friends it just made me miss them even more.'

'I reckon the best way to feel better is to start making some new friends,' said Amelia. 'It doesn't mean you won't miss your old friends, but at least you won't be alone.'

'I guess so.' Harry smiled and followed the girls over to Matthew and Arlo to play soccer.

'Hey, Arlo. Can Harry play?' asked Helen.

'Of course!' said Arlo. 'He's a good guy, aren't you, Harry? It's not like you're a graffiti bandit, is it?'

Amelia and her friends looked at each other and burst out laughing.